Hamish and the Wee Witch

'Whigmaleeries!' shrieked the furious wee witch,
gasping for breath. 'I'll make you sorry about this. I
will that! You'll live to regret this or . . . or my
name's not – GRIZELDA GRIMITHISTLE!'

MOIRA MILLER

Hamish
and the
Wee Witch

Illustrated by Mairi Hedderwick

CANONGATE
KELPIES

Also by Moira Miller
Hamish and the Fairy Gifts

If you enjoyed this Kelpie and would like a free
Kelpie sticker and catalogue please contact:

Customer Services
Canongate Books Ltd
14 High Street
Edinburgh EH1 1TE

First published in Great Britain in 1986
by Methuen Children's Books Ltd
Published in Kelpies 1995

Text Copyright © Moira Miller 1986
Illustrations copyright © Mairi Hedderwick 1986

British Library Cataloguing-in-Publication Data
A catalogue record of this book is available upon request from
the British Library.

ISBN 0 86241 566 7

Printed and bound in Denmark by Norhaven A/S

Contents

1
Hamish and the Big Wind

It was a beautiful late summer evening. The sun had shone all day, warm and golden on the hayfield, dazzling on the little white cottage and dancing, sparkling and silver on the sea loch.

It was setting now in a glowing scarlet ball, filling the cottage kitchen with rosy light.

Hamish stretched his long legs out across the hearthrug, yawned and wiggled his toes in his socks.

'You great big clumsy tumshie!' grumbled his old mother, tripping over his feet. 'Mind what you're doing.' She leaned across him to stir the soup in the iron pot over the fire.

Hamish chuckled. He was happy after a good day's work, and even his old mother's scolding was not going to change that. From the crisp early morning mist to the long golden evening he had worked in the two green fields that ran from the farmhouse down to the shore of the loch. The rich grass he had cut and spread to dry in the sun was now piled up into two neat round haystacks by the byre. The animals would feed well through the long, cold winter months. Everything on the farm was quiet and peaceful. Just as it should be.

So Hamish stretched out his legs, rumpled his fair hair until it stood up like a corn stook above his rosy face, and smiled contentedly.

But not for long.

WHOOSH!

Suddenly with a crash and a cloud of black smoke a great wind blew down the chimney into the room. The cat shot off the rug and ran squawking under the table. Hamish's old mother coughed and screeched and threw her apron over her face. The wind howled round the kitchen toppling cups and plates on the dresser, slammed the door open and stormed, roaring with laughter, out into the yard.

'Come back here, you great Hooligan!' roared Hamish, struggling to pull on his boots. He tumbled out after the wind, and what a sight met his eyes.

The wooden bucket clattered noisily round and round on the cobble-stoned yard. The hen house, blown over on its

side, was a screeching mass of feathers.
The door of the byre crashed to and fro
madly on its old hinges. Worst of all – the
two neat round haystacks had gone.

Blown clear away with the Big Wind.

'What a mixter-maxter!' gasped Hamish,
grabbing the bucket as it trundled past. He
set to work to clear up, and all the time he
raged about his haystacks.

'I'll get them back though,' he growled.
'Never you fear.'

His old mother sniffed and shook her
head.

'I doubt your haystacks will be over the
hills and far away by now,' she said.
'You'll never catch the Big Wind.'

'Will I not?' said Hamish. 'We'll soon
see about that.'

He pulled on his jerkin, took the stout
leather bag that hung behind the door and
filled it with bread, meat and cheese. He
tied it firmly round the top with a length
of rope and kissed his mother goodbye.

'What about your soup?' she shouted
after him.

'Keep it till I get back,' called Hamish.
'WITH the haystacks.'

She shook her head as she watched him

march off through the heather up across the hill, following the path the wind had blown.

For miles and miles he walked, over high windswept moorland. He had finished most of the bread and had no meat or cheese left when he came upon a lonely farm cottage.

'Have you seen a Big Wind pass this way?' Hamish asked of the farmer.

The man stopped digging and leaned on his spade.

'Would that be the wind,' said he, 'that came by here the other night and made away with the thatched roof of my cowshed?'

'The very one,' said Hamish. 'He's away with my two round haystacks and I'm after fetching them back. It may be that I can help you too.'

'Then good luck to you, laddie,' said the farmer. 'For it's the long cold road you have to follow. You'll stop and have a bite to eat with us first.'

Hamish set off again with his bag once more full of food. He walked on and on across hillside and glen, by river and loch until he came to a mill.

'Have you seen a Big Wind pass this way?' Hamish asked of the miller.

The man put down the heavy bag of grain he was carrying and stood up, stretching his back.

'Would that be the wind,' said he, 'that came by here the other night and made away with my wheelbarrow?'

'The very one,' said Hamish. 'He's away with my two round haystacks and I'm after fetching them back. It may be that I can help you too.'

'Then good luck to you, laddie,' said the miller. 'For it's the long cold road you have to follow. You'll stop and have a bite to eat with me first.'

Having eaten and rested Hamish set off once more and came at last to a little dairy by the roadside. In the cool white kitchen a young girl was stirring cream in a big wooden churn to make butter.

'Have you seen a Big Wind pass this way?' Hamish asked of the dairymaid.

'Would that be the wind,' said she, 'that whistled through my garden the other night and made away with my best petticoat from the washing line?'

'The very one,' said Hamish. 'He's

taken my two round haystacks and I'm after fetching them back. It may be that I can help you too.' The dairymaid looked him up and down, and giggled.

'Then you're the very lad they're looking for up at the castle,' said she. 'The Laird himself has offered a rich reward to the man who can catch the Big Wind.'

'Indeed?' said Hamish.

'Half his gold and silver,' said the dairymaid.

'Fancy that!' said Hamish.

'And one of his daughters to marry,' sniffed the dairymaid. 'Hoity toity misses!' Hamish laughed, gave her a kiss and a cuddle and asked the way to the castle.

In the great hall the Laird sat at dinner with his three daughters. The two older ones ignored Hamish completely, but the youngest one, with long golden pigtails and freckles like new pennies, offered him a stool and a cup of wine.

'That's the way, Mirren,' said the Laird. 'Come away in, laddie. Sit down and give us your crack.' He listened carefully while Hamish told the story of his haystacks, and how he was determined to win them back again, along with the reward.

'Aye, well,' said the Laird, 'there's some fine young men have come after the reward. And gone home again in a very sorry state . . . very sorry indeed . . . ' He shook his head and stared gloomily at his daughters.

'Och, father,' said the oldest one, 'they were none of them grand enough to marry US anyway.'

'One day,' said the second daughter looking down her nose at Hamish, 'a *REAL* prince will come and claim the reward – and *MY* hand in marriage.' She stared dreamily into her pudding.

'He will not!' screamed the first daughter, thumping the table till the plates jumped. 'He'll want *ME*.' The Laird sighed, shook his head and led Hamish over to the window.

The old grey stone castle stood on a cliff top overlooking the sea, which lapped grey and cold on the rocks beneath them.

'Do you see yon island out there?' said the Laird. Through the evening mirk Hamish could just make out the jagged shape of a small island in the bay.

Looming above the rocks, and seeming almost to have grown from them, there stood an old ruined tower.

'I see it,' said Hamish.

'Then that's where the Big Wind is to be found,' said the Laird. 'When he's not out and about stirring up a shindig like that pair there!' At the table his two older daughters were still squabbling.

Hamish laughed and winked at Mirren.

'Leave this to me,' said he. 'I'll soon see him off!' The Laird offered Hamish a suit of armour for protection, but it was so long since it had been used that the hinges were rusted solid. Mirren found him an old helmet, but Hamish only roared with laughter.

'It's big enough to make soup for the village in!' Taking only a small boat and his big leather bag he rowed himself out to the island, and slept that night on the beach.

He awoke with the first light of day, stretched and sat up — and what a surprise met him then. In the still morning the island held its breath. There was no sign of the Big Wind, but tumbled all about him lay gates and fences, shed roofs and wheelbarrows. Amongst them, with the dairymaid's petticoat draped on top, were his two neat round haystacks.

Hamish was struggling to load them into the boat when the sky suddenly darkened.

There came a distant whistling and roaring like a huge dragon. The sea around the island tossed and boiled, the waves twisted and crashed on the pebble beach. In a great swirling of spray the Big Wind shrieked across the island.

'Oooooooo-hoooooooo!' he roared. 'And where do you think you're going with these, young sir?'

'Taking them home, where they belong,' said Hamish calmly, carrying on as if nothing had happened.

'O-oh-ho, you're not!' roared the Big Wind.

'O-oh-ho, yes I AM!' said Hamish. 'And you can puff till you're blue in the face, but you'll not stop me.'

The Big Wind, whipped to a frenzy, whirled himself into a huge black cloud and raged down. Hamish dropped the hay and jumped neatly aside. The Wind crashed into the wall behind him.

'Can't catch me for a wee bawbee!' sang Hamish rudely. The Big Wind gathered himself into a screaming rage.

Then there followed such a racing and chasing all around that island and the ruined tower. Hamish jumped in and out of doorways, up and down stairways, in and out through empty windows, with the Big Wind in pursuit. But wherever the Big Wind pounced, Hamish had been – and gone.

'Stand still you cheeky wee limmer!' roared the Wind, whirling into a hurricane.

'Now I'm here, now I'm there,
But you canna catch me anywhere,'

sang Hamish.

He dodged laughing and panting into the hall of the old tower. In front of him the huge fireplace stood, black and empty, and at his heels the Big Wind screamed in fury. Hamish looked quickly round the room.

There was nowhere to turn.

'Aaaaaaaa-haaaaa, I've got you now!' shrieked the Big Wind. 'Just wait till I catch hold of you!'

Hamish ran for the fireplace, dodging and weaving, and scrambled up the great empty chimney. Higher and higher, faster and faster he climbed until at last he struggled out at the top, gasping for breath. Behind him the Big Wind snatched at his heels.

Quick as a flash Hamish grabbed his leather bag, opened it wide, and held it over the chimney top.

'Ooooooooo-hoooooooo!' roared the Big Wind in terrifying triumph – and whistled straight into Hamish's big leather bag. It was a second's work for him to tie the rope with three tight knots and stuff the bag back into the chimney. As he climbed back down the outside of the old tower he could hear the wind howling and struggling to be set free.

When the story of how Hamish had tricked the Big Wind became known, people came from far and wide to claim their stolen belongings. Some of them just came to look at the tower and listen to the Wind howling in the chimney. They were shown round the island by the Laird's two older daughters, who had moved across to live there.

'Because after all,' said the oldest, 'one of these days a *REAL* prince might come sightseeing. Who knows? And when he does come he'll fall in love with me – on the instant . . . '

'RUBBISH!' screamed the younger one, stamping her foot. 'How could he possibly – you ugly old bat!'

All day long their voices echoed round the island and faintly back across the sea to where the Laird sat smiling peacefully in his castle.

Mirren smiled too. She smiled and tossed her long pigtails and said 'yes' when Hamish asked to marry her. The party lasted for a month and a day, with feasting and dancing in the castle and the village. Even the dairymaid, who was invited, had to admit that Hamish had chosen a beautiful bride – who was not in the least bit stuck up.

After a time, however, Hamish began to miss his home, so one fine morning he and Mirren said goodbye to the Laird, who would have been very unhappy had it not been for the fact that the dairymaid had agreed to stay on at the castle as his housekeeper.

Hamish and Mirren packed all their belongings, loaded the neat round haystacks into a cart, and set off back to the wee farmhouse and the two green fields that ran down to the shining silver sea loch.

2
Hamish and the Wee Witch

Hamish and Mirren came home to the farm, all set to live happily ever after.

But sometimes things don't work out like that.

Mirren loved the little white house on the hillside. Every morning she ran out into the fields where the fresh taste of the sea mingled with the warm smell of the wild flowers. She laughed to see how the fat brown hens came running to greet her.

'Here, here. Chook chook chook,' she called, scattering corn like golden rain from the big basket. The hens fussed around her feet pecking and squabbling as she called to them. The eggs they laid for Mirren seemed bigger and browner and the yolks more golden than ever before.

'Mmmmm, she's no' bad – for a laird's daughter,' sniffed Hamish's old mother. 'But do you think she can milk a cow?'

Hamish laughed as he watched Mirren dance round the farmyard among the hens.

'Of course she can!' he said. 'My wee Mirren can do anything.' And he was just about right. Very soon Mirren was milking the cow as well and the big wooden bucket was filled to the top every day with rich creamy milk.

'You're a treasure,' said Hamish, 'and I wouldna' change you for all the gold and silver in your father's kists.'

Mirren laughed and went on about her work, singing like the thrush in the hawthorn bush. Even Hamish's old mother had to admit that the farm was a brighter and happier place.

It seemed as if it would always be like that, and they would live happily ever after but suddenly one day, there came a change.

Mirren stopped singing.

She came in from the byre after the morning milking with the big wooden pail only half full.

'Och, Mirren,' said Hamish. 'Is the wee cow not well?'

'I don't know,' said Mirren, puzzled and upset. 'She seems restless and unhappy, and though I begged for more that was all the milk she had to give.'

'Well never mind Mirren,' said Hamish. 'Maybe she'll do better in the morn, and if anyone can help her, you can.'

But the next morning it was the same

story. The wee cow only gave half a bucket of milk, and that so thin and weak it might as well have been water from the loch.

Mirren was very unhappy.

'No sense in crying over the milk,' said Hamish trying to comfort her. 'I'll see what I can do.' That evening he took the bucket and went out to the byre.

As he stepped from the back door into the yard he was just in time to hear a scuffling sound, and catch a glimpse of a little old woman in a green cloak. In her hurry to leave she caught the cloak on a nail by the byre door.

'Whigmaleeries!' she hooted, and pulled at the cloth to free herself. As she did so Hamish could see that she was carrying a wooden pail. And that pail was full to the brim with rich creamy milk.

'Here!' called Hamish running after her. 'That's my milk you're after stealing.' The little old woman whirled round and fixed him with a bright beady green eye.

'Away ye go,' she croaked, pointing a finger like a twisted twig, 'or I'll turn you into a toad!'

Hamish stepped back into the cottage and slammed the door shut as she vanished in a cloud of evil-smelling black smoke.

'We have to stop her,' he said to his mother and Mirren as they sat down to supper later that evening. 'But how?'

Mirren shook her head, she was at a loss to know what to do. Hamish turned to his mother. She was older and wiser and knew about these things.

'That woman is one of the Wee Folk,' she said. 'And it'll no' be easy to stop her, I'm thinking. But there is a way.' She got up and looked quickly round the cottage – under the table, and up the chimney – then closing the door tight shut she came back and sat down.

'I've never tried it myself,' she whispered, 'but they do say that if you can find out the name of a wee witch then she'll have no power to cast a spell over you.'

'Then we must find her name,' said Mirren, 'and send her back where she came from.'

But that was not so easy. For days she and Hamish went round their neighbours asking if anyone knew of the old woman. They found that although she had stolen eggs from this one, and butter from that nobody could help. They, none of them, knew who she was.

'We'll go down to Camusbuie,' said Hamish. 'There may be someone in the village who can help.' But even old Biddy who kept the shop and knew all the gossip before it happened, was no help at all.

And every day the wee old witch came back to fill her bucket with stolen milk.

At last Hamish's old mother had had enough. She liked nothing better than the rich creamy milk with a plate of porridge and she was missing it very much.

She put down her spoon with a bang on the breakfast table. Hamish and Mirren jumped.

'I'll soon sort this out,' she said. Pulling her shawl tightly round her she stamped out to the byre.

'Here, mother!' shouted Hamish running after her. 'She'll do something terrible!'

'Just let her try!' sniffed Hamish's mother. She slammed open the byre door, and there sure enough, sat the wee old witch. She was perched on the old milking stool, rocking gently from side to side and crooning a strange song as she milked the wee cow into her big bucket.

'Out of there, you!' screamed Hamish's mother. 'You can't even milk a cow properly. Look at the way you're doing it – all back side hindmost. No wonder the poor beast's upset!' She barged in knocking the old witch off her milking stool.

Hamish jumped back out of the way as she rolled over at his feet in a dirty green bundle.

'How dare you!' howled the old witch, her feet waving in the air. 'I've been milking cows for three hundred and forty nine years. Are you trying to tell me I don't know what I'm doing?'

'Just that,' said Hamish's mother firmly. 'Now get out of the way and let me get on with it.'

The wee old witch staggered to her feet, her face purple with rage, her straggly hair stuck full of straw.

'I'll turn you into a toad!' she screamed, struggling to get up again.

'Aye, well if you're as good at that as you are at milking, I'll not be too bothered,' said Hamish's mother, calmly sitting down on the milking stool.

'Whigmaleeries!' shrieked the furious wee witch, gasping for breath. 'I'll make you sorry about this. I will that! You'll live to regret this or . . . or my name's not –GRIZELDA GRIMITHISTLE!'

There was silence.

Hamish stared at his mother, who smiled and nodded.

'Grizelda Grimithistle is it? Well, well, fancy that,' she said smugly.

Hamish roared with laughter at the sight of the wee witch's face.

'Much obliged to you for telling us, Grizelda Grimithistle,' he said. 'And now that we know, you'll not be stealing any more milk.'

'You can forget the eggs and butter from down the road too,' said his mother.

The wee old witch was livid with fury. She screamed and stamped and spun round in such a temper that she rolled herself into a huge green ball. Still screeching and howling she whirled out of the byre and up over the hill, burning a path through the heather that is still there to this day.

Down in Camusbuie they said afterwards that her howls could be heard clear across the Seven Glens and the echoes rolled like thunder round the top of the Ben of Balvie all that day.

'I don't doubt we've seen the last of Grizelda Grimithistle on this farm,' said Hamish's old mother as she picked up the bucket full of rich creamy milk for her porridge.

And so they had – well almost.

3
Hamish and the Pedlar's Pipe

Hamish and Mirren had been down in the village of Camusbuie for the day. Hamish had sold all his cheese and butter, and bought a fine new iron pot to hang on the hook over the fire. Mirren had sold her eggs and the soft woollen shawls that Hamish's old mother had knitted during the long winter months. She had bought herself a red woollen skirt and they were singing as they marched back up the road home.

The path they took wound up from the village, round the heather-covered shoulder of the Ben of Balvie. The Ben was so high that there were days, even in summer, when the top was hidden in thick white clouds. But now the sun was shining and the Ben stood crisp against the pure blue of a cloudless sky.

Mirren ran through the long grass by the path, picking wild flowers. Meadowsweet and buttercup she gathered by the armful.

Suddenly she stopped and stood quite still.

'What is it?' called Hamish from the path behind her.

'Shhhh,' said Mirren. 'Can you not hear it?'

They stood together on the quiet sunlit path. At first Hamish heard nothing, but then Mirren smiled.

'Listen,' she whispered. From far off, away beyond the happy chirping of the birds, came a strange little tune, silvery and clear.

The music was slow and gentle, and although it was far off, at the same time it seemed to be all around them. It whispered, dancing like the butterflies through the trees and the thick green grass. It was hard to tell whether the tune was sad or happy – or both. Mirren stood spellbound.

'My, it's that bonny,' she whispered.

'It's the Wee Folk,' said Hamish and he held tight to his new iron pot. Everyone knows that if you have something of iron about you then the Wee Folk are unable to weave their spells.

'No,' laughed Mirren. 'It's just a travelling pedlar. Look!'

Sure enough, round the corner of the

path, down from the Ben came a strange figure.

He seemed tall at first, but then Hamish noticed he was not much bigger than Mirren. He wore a long brown swirling cloak that seemed almost to float behind him. A huge shady brown hat with a curling feather hid most of his face.

Under the brim of the hat they could see that his hair was thick and dark, and that his bright brown eyes seemed to dance and twinkle in time with his music.

The stranger was playing the haunting music on a thin silver pipe.

'Fine evening,' called Hamish. 'You fair startled us. That's a rare tune you're playing.'

'Ah, it's the fine flute, sir, that does it,' said the pedlar. He stopped on the path in front of them and smiled with his head tilted to one side. 'I could sell you this for just one of those six gold coins you earned today.'

'How did you know about the gold?' said Hamish, but the pedlar ignored him and turned smiling to Mirren.

'It will make music to have your old slippers dancing on the hearthrug,' he said. 'And the birds themselves will stop singing to listen.' He put the flute to his lips again and trilled a tune like a blackbird's. Fine clear notes that tumbled over each other in sheer happiness.

'My, but that is bonny,' whispered Mirren.

'Here,' said the pedlar. 'Take it, and welcome.'

Before Hamish knew what had happened he was standing with the pipe in his hand and the pedlar was off down the path with one of his gold coins.

'Just a minute,' Hamish shouted after him. 'I can't play this. Tell me – how do I make music with it?'

The pedlar turned back, laughing.

'That's a gift that's given to the man with a kind heart,' he called, 'and the breath to blow clear through the Ben of Balvie.'

'Blow through the Ben?' shouted Hamish, angry now. 'Yon's not possible! Here you – give me my money back . . . '

But the pedlar had vanished and

although Hamish and Mirren searched high and low through the trees and along the path all they saw was the dancing lace of the shadows. All they heard was the sweet song of the birds.

'Never mind, Hamish,' said Mirren at last. 'Maybe you can learn how to play the wee pipe yourself.'

'Aye, maybe,' sighed Hamish. He put the pipe to his lips and blew, but the only sound that came out was a high piercing whistle that hurt the ears.

Night after night Hamish sat by the fire blowing at his pipe. Mirren tried as well. But there was no way they could make music as the pedlar had.

'Mercy on us,' screeched his old mother. 'That's more like a parcel of cats fighting in the barn! Put the thing away laddie, afore we're all deaf.'

Sadly, Hamish put the little pipe in his pouch and forgot all about it – until some weeks later.

It happened that he was up on the slopes of the Ben of Balvie, bringing down his sheep, when he remembered the pipe again.

'It can hardly bother anyone if I play it

up here,' he said to himself. The shining silver of the little pipe was dull, from having lain forgotten in his pouch. Hamish breathed on it, and rubbed it on his shirt sleeve.

He took a deep breath, put the pipe to his lips, and blew. But though he blew until his face was red as the sunset and there was no puff left in him, the little silver pipe only squeaked and howled as before.

'Good gracious, laddie, what a cater-wauling,' came a voice behind him.

Hamish spun round, and came face to face with a wee old woman. Smaller than his own mother, but plumper, she stood in the heather with a large round bundle wrapped in an old green shawl at her feet.

'Where did you come from?' said Hamish. 'I don't mind seeing you on the path.'

'Aye, well seen that,' said the old woman. Then she smiled at him. 'You look like a big strong lad. Before you blow yourself clean to bits, I'd be much obliged if you could give me a wee bit help. I've been on a visit to my grandson and now I find I'm locked out of my house.'

'No trouble,' said Hamish. 'You lead me there, and I'll soon get you in.'

'It's this way,' said the wee old woman. 'Follow me.' She picked up her skirts and set off climbing towards the top of the Ben.

'And bring my bundle with you!' she called back.

'Aye, right,' laughed Hamish, swinging it up onto his shoulder. His knees buckled as he almost sank under the weight.

'How did you ever manage to lift this?' he gasped, amazed. But the wee old woman was away, striding ahead of him. Hamish hoisted the bundle onto his broad shoulder and set off after her.

Higher and higher they climbed up the rocky slope. There was no sign of house or cottage but the wee old woman marched on so Hamish had to follow. Up among the mist and clouds they climbed. With the damp striking cold through his shirt and the bundle becoming heavier and heavier, Hamish staggered to a halt, panting.

'Guidsakes, laddie,' fussed the old woman coming back down through the mist. 'Pick up your feet will you. We'll never get there this night!'

Wearily Hamish dragged the bundle up again and stumbled on. At last, just as the last of his strength had gone and he knew he could climb no further, the old woman stopped and turned to him.

'Right laddie, we're here now,' she said. 'Set it down, careful mind! There's things in that shawl that all the riches in the world could never buy.'

Hamish gently lowered the bundle and stared around. In front of him the bleak rocky mountainside vanished into the mist. To the right a great slope of small stones and gravel swept down like a waterfall of rock, and to his left rose a sheer cliff face.

'Are you sure this is where you live?' he gasped, amazed.

'Do you think I don't know my own front door?' sniffed the old woman indignantly. 'Now you take out that pipe, laddie, and blow. Blow as long and as loud as ever you can.'

Hamish took out his silver pipe, drew in a deep breath, and blew.

He blew a fine high piercing note that

could have been heard clear over the Ben and down to Camusbuie. The note echoed up the hillside and rang back off the rocks, louder and louder, as if it would never stop.

And in the high clear ringing tone of the flute, the rocks in front of Hamish seemed to melt away. The grey towering cliff face dissolved into a deep cave lit by a soft green shimmering light.

Hamish stopped blowing, and stood open-mouthed as the echoes died around him.

The wee old woman nodded, picked up her bundle as if it had been light as a feather, and stepped into the cave. Around her, shadowy silvery figures came and went, flitting soundlessly.

The woman who turned back to Hamish was no longer old. She was young, and beautiful, and smiling.

'Aye, we did right to give you that pipe,' she chuckled. 'You've a kind heart and the breath to blow clear through the Ben. Now away home with you and blow your pipe. Blow it for all the world to hear.'

The green light of the cave faded.

Hamish blinked, and found himself staring at the grey rocks. A wisp of cloud trailed across the cliff face, and the sun broke through, warming his back.

He turned then and ran, leaping from stone to stone, slipping and sliding, panting for breath. Away from the cloud-wrapped top of the Ben he ran, back down the mountainside. At last he tumbled onto the grassy slope above the path that led to home, and lay panting. The sun, breaking through the patch in the clouds, suddenly shone down on Camusbuie, the loch and his tiny white house far below.

Hamish picked himself up brushing the grass from his clothes.

'I doubt I must have been dreaming,' he said, shaking his head. It would have taken hours to climb the Ben, and above his head the sun was still high in the sky.

He laughed and set off to walk down the grassy slope. As he went he took the silver pipe from his pouch, put it to his lips and blew.

By the time he reached the cottage his

fingers were skipping on the little flute to a tune that would have made your old slippers dance on the hearthrug.

Even the very birds in the trees had stopped singing to listen in wonder.

4
Mirren and the Spring Cleaning

It all started because Mirren was in a bit of a bad mood.

She had been working on the farm, and in the byre , and what with one thing and another had not been able to make a start on the spring cleaning in the cottage.

One night, when Hamish's old mother had gone off to bed early, he and Mirren were peacefully toasting their toes in front of the fire. Hamish yawned and stretched. Mirren, who had been fidgeting in her chair all evening, suddenly jumped up.

'If I don't start now,' she said, 'it'll never get done!' She grabbed the broom and swept the rug so hard that great clouds of dust flew up around her. Hamish sneezed and the cat shot off under the corner cupboard.

'Here Mirren,' panted Hamish, between sneezes. 'It's far too late for that. Nobody does a spring cleaning at bedtime.'

'Stuff!' said Mirren, lifting the rug and shaking it.

'Aaaaaaaa-chooo!' Hamish gave a sneeze that rattled the china dogs on the mantelpiece.

'You can sit there till the cows come home if you like,' said Mirren. 'But this spring cleaning is going to get done.'

Hamish sat on by the fire for a time as she polished and dusted around him. He shifted his chair three times so that Mirren could sweep underneath it. When she rolled up her sleeves and filled a bucket of water Hamish decided that he had had enough.

'I think I'll leave you to get on with it,' he said, tiptoeing through the puddles. 'I'm away to bed.'

But Mirren heard never a word. She was scrubbing and polishing as though her life depended on it.

She took down all the curtains and left them to soak in a tub of clean water. She shook up the old patchwork cushions until the feathers flew like a snowstorm. She scrubbed and rubbed at the best copper kettle until her own face was smiling back, round and golden brown, with the one wee dimple where the kettle had a dent in it.

It was while she was polishing the face of the old wag-at-the-wa' clock that Mirren suddenly realised that the time was almost midnight.

In the big bedroom Hamish was snoring softly, while in the wee room at the back his old mother muttered something to herself in her sleep, turned over and settled down again.

Mirren looked around her. There still seemed so much to be done. In the quietness of the night the big clock chimed twelve. Mirren dried her hands, stretched her back, and sighed.

'Oh that someone would come,
From land or sea,
From far or near
With help for me.'

Now at midnight that is a dangerous thing to do, for the Wee Folk are always around somewhere – and always listening. And that was just the sort of invitation they could never resist.

No sooner had Mirren said the words, and the twelfth chime, still echoing round the little room, than there was a knock on the door.

'Mercy on us,' Mirren jumped. 'Who can that be at this time of the night.'

'Open the door to me, Mirren my lass,' came a strange voice. 'You begged for help and the time that I have will be yours alone.'

Mirren opened the door, just a crack, and came face to face with a fat little man.

His untidy white beard half hid a face that was crinkled and brown like a walnut. He hitched up his baggy brown tunic, and before Mirren could say another word had shoved open the door and stepped into the cottage.

'Aye,' he said, glancing round and pushing up his sleeves. 'We'll soon have you set to rights, lass.' He grabbed the bucket of water and set to, scrubbing the floor all over again.

'Here, stop, I've done that . . . ' Mirren started to say when there came another knock at the door. In barged two old women wearing green aprons and big wooden clogs. They snatched the cushions from the chairs and plumped and pulled at them.

'Stop it!' yelled Mirren, trying to grab

the cushions. But she might as well have been talking to the clock.

After that came another knock at the door, then another and another, until at last the whole house was full of Wee Folk all falling over each other, kicking over buckets of water, knocking over ornaments and generally creating a shambles in the tidy little kitchen.

Mirren stared in horror. She raced into the bedroom and shook Hamish, but he was deep asleep. The harder she shook him, the louder he snored. It was as if he slept the sleep of the enchanted.

'Please,' she begged the Wee Folk. 'Please will you stop!'

'Aye, well,' said one of the old ladies. 'I wouldn't mind a wee cup of tea about now.'

Mirren quickly stirred up the fire and set the kettle to boil.

'I'll just have the buttermilk,' said the little old man who had arrived first.

'Try some of the shortbread,' screeched another voice. 'It's not bad – considering.'

Before Mirren could stop them, the Wee Folk had eaten and drunk everything they could lay their hands on. Even the porridge that Mirren had put to simmer for breakfast by the side of the fire had gone.

And no sooner was it finished than they went back to work with a will, scrubbing and polishing like mad things. One wee woman grabbed the big wooden bucket in which the curtains were soaking and started to scrub down the cupboard with them.

'No – no!' howled Mirren, trying to pull the bucket away, but the wee woman held on tightly.

'It's no trouble, lassie,' she screeched. 'I like to see a job well done.' She dunked the curtains back in the dirty water, soaking herself and Mirren, and went on scrubbing.

Mirren was desperate. She had to stop them somehow before they ruined her little home – but how.

'Hamish's mother!' she whispered to herself. Like many old people Hamish's mother seemed to know more about the Wee Folk than most.

The old lady lay on her back, a big white frilly nightcap pulled down over

her hair, and a soft knitted shawl about her shoulders. Mirren shook her gently.

'Eh – eh . . . two plain, two purl . . . ' muttered the old lady. Mirren shook her a little harder. The old lady snuffled like a hedgehog and turned over on her side.

'Please, mother, wake up,' hissed Mirren. 'It's the Wee Folk. I can't get rid of them.'

Hamish's mother sat up and pulled the shawl tight around her shoulders. She listened as Mirren told her what had happened.

'Aye well, if you did your spring cleaning in the daytime like the rest of the world . . . ' said the old lady. Mirren sniffed into her handkerchief.

'I can't get them out of the house,' she wailed. 'They won't go until they've finished.'

'We'll soon see about that,' said Hamish's mother. 'You slip out the back door, and stand on that wee bit hillock over by the hawthorn tree. Then when I wave you'll shout – as loud as you can, mind now.'

'But what do I shout?' asked Mirren.

'I'm coming to that,' said the old lady

crossly. 'You'll shout 'Dun Shee is on fire!' Shout three times, loud and clear. That'll soon get them out.'

'But why? What's Dun Shee?' asked Mirren perplexed.

'Bless me,' said the old lady. 'Don't you know anything? Dun Shee is the name they have for their own Fairy Hill where they live. If they think it's on fire they'll be out of this house quicker than you can wink!'

So Mirren did as she was told. She crept quietly out of the back door and climbed the wee hillock. Around her the night sky was dark and still – even the stars slept. Behind her, from inside the cottage, she could hear the crashing, banging and yells of the Wee Folk.

Mirren took a deep breath and shouted at the top of her voice.

'Dun Shee is on fire! Dun Shee is on fire! Dun Shee is on fire!'

Out they rushed, falling over each other in their hurry. Screeching and squawking like hens with a fox after them, scattering brooms, buckets and dusters as they went. They tumbled off up the hill in a great noisy green whirlwind.

Mirren waited until she was sure the last one had gone. She ran back into the cottage, bolted the door behind her and pushed the big kitchen table across the front to jam it shut.

'It worked!' she panted. 'They've gone. We've done it.'

'Aye, but they'll be back, mark my words,' said Hamish's mother. 'And they'll be ill-pleased when they find we've tricked them. But we'll be ready for them — we'll be ready.'

No sooner had she said that than there came a sound like a great rushing of wind and a pounding on the door.

'Let us in, Mirren. Let us in!' called the voices. 'We've not done yet, and you'll not keep us out.'

'Go away!' shouted Mirren. 'Oh please go away!'

But the voices went on calling, kicking and pounding on the door.

'Let us in!' echoed the voices down the chimney. Hamish's mother stirred the fire to a blaze and piled on more peat, stirring up the smoke. Outside there was coughing and sneezing – and then silence.

'What are they doing do you think?' whispered Mirren.

Suddenly the broom jumped up from the rug and swept round the room in a mad dance.

'So that's the way it's to be,' said Hamish's mother. 'Mirren, fetch some of those big iron nails that Hamish used to mend the fence. Hurry now.'

Mirren found the bag of nails and the big hammer.

'Right now,' said the old woman. 'The Wee Folk can never cast a spell where there is cold iron. You put a nail in the handle of that broom.'

But that was easier said than done. The broom jinked and jouked around the furniture, behind the cupboards, and even into the bedroom. Mirren chased after it, climbing over the bed, and still Hamish slept on, snoring gently. At last she trapped the broom in a corner of the kitchen.

'Quickly!' she shouted. 'The hammer.' She held on grimly as the broom danced madly round the room dragging her with it. Hamish's mother grabbed the handle and in the end it took the two of them to get it down onto the floor. They sat one on each end while Mirren banged in a nail.

The broom lay still and quiet and as ordinary as it had ever been.

Mirren sat on the floor, puffing and panting. Before she had time to catch her breath, however, the dusters started up. They flew round the room rubbing and polishing everything they touched – the table, the cupboard, the mantelpiece.

'Get off!' screeched the old lady as they flew at her like great coloured seagulls. Mirren leapt and jumped, trying to catch them. The clock was polished so hard it chimed thirteen times, and still they flew round and round the room.

'The kist!' shouted the old woman, catching one of the china dogs as it fell from the mantelpiece. 'Get them into the kist! It's made of rowan wood, and the Wee Folk's magic can't abide that.'

The dusters by this time were rolling about beneath the big cupboard, fighting like a pair of cats. Mirren poked at them with a knitting pin.

'I've got them,' she yelled, grabbing a handful of cloth. The old woman opened the lid of the big rowan-wood chest and Mirren stuffed two of the dusters in. The third duster, twisting out of her hand, flew crazily round the room above their heads.

Mirren swiped at it with the broom. The old woman stood on the stool and screeched at it to come down immediately. The duster flapped round cheekily, just out of reach.

At last Mirren managed to jump high enough to grab a corner. She pulled it over to the chest, opened the lid just a crack, and stuffing it in, flopped down breathless on top. In the quiet room the only sounds were the old clock and her gasping breath.

Outside, the night was over.

The early morning filled the sky with a clear pearly blue. The cockerel called from the yard and the cows mooed softly to each other in the byre.

Far off in the distance the gentle sea lapped on the beach and down by the village a dog barked as the first threads of smoke snaked lazily up from cottage chimneys.

'Have they gone?' whispered Mirren hoarsely.

'Aye,' said the old woman. 'But they've had their fun.'

Mirren and the old lady flopped down in the chairs by the fireside, exhausted, as the early morning sun creeping through the windows lit the tiny kitchen, and filled the bedroom with brightness.

Hamish woke at last, stretched and yawned.

'My, that was a rare sleep,' he called through to Mirren as he dressed. 'I don't know when . . . '

And then he stood – and stopped, and stared.

He stared at his mother and Mirren, sound asleep on either side of the cold fireplace.

He stared at the empty porridge pot tipped on the floor.

He stared in amazement at the sink full of dirty dishes and the little kitchen, usually so tidy, and now such a shambles.

'Mirren,' he gasped. 'What on earth have you been doing all night?'

Mirren stirred, then settled herself more comfortably in the big chair.

'Spring cleaning,' she muttered – and went back to sleep again.

5
Hamish and the Sea Urchin

The weather had been wild and stormy for days. The wind played a mad dance in the trees around Hamish's farmhouse and whistled down the chimney into the fireplace so that the flames flickered and jumped unevenly round the bottom of the iron kettle.

Every night, as they lay snug in bed, Hamish and Mirren listened to the sea roaring on the rocks.

'I don't like it,' whispered Mirren in the dark.

'Och, it's just the Spring tides,' said Hamish. 'It happens every year. The tide comes up further and further each day – but then it goes out further as well. One day it'll go out as far as it can and then after that it will come back to being the same as always. You'll see, Mirren, don't worry. Go to sleep.'

Mirren lay and listened to the huge waves crashing on the rocks and tearing at the seaweed on the shore, and she pulled the big blanket up over her head and went back to sleep.

Early next morning she yawned and stretched.

After the days of stormy weather the sun was shining again, the wild screaming wind had gone. Everything was still. There was no sound – not even the waves crashing on the beach.

Mirren leapt out of bed and ran to the window.

'Hamish, come quick!' she called. 'The sea's gone. It's not there any more. What's happened? Hamish, wake up, you dozy lump. What's happened?'

Hamish climbed out of bed sleepily and came to the window. Before the house, instead of the silver sheet of the loch stretching away between the hills to the distant shimmering blue line of the sea, there was only sand. Miles and miles of shining wet sand.

'My, the tide's fairly gone out this time,' said Hamish, scratching his head. 'There's rocks out there I've never seen before.'

'Fancy that,' whispered Mirren.

'Nobody's ever set foot out there,' said Hamish. 'I've a mind to do it myself before the tide comes back in, just to say I've walked down the loch.'

'It isn't safe,' grumbled his old mother over breakfast. Hamish laughed and took a stout walking stick from the basket by the door.

'Don't say I didn't warn you,' she grumbled, stumping back to her chair by the fireside.

But Hamish was away, striding out across the wet sand, stopping now and then to look at the things the sea had left behind as it swept out of the loch. He picked up a pretty pebble and put it in his pouch for Mirren. Then on he went again, across the wet firm sand, leaving footprints where no footprints had ever been seen before.

Out towards the middle of the loch where the sand was softest lay a clump of black weed-covered rocks. Hamish clambered over the slippery surface, searching in pools and cracks for the tiny plants and sea creatures normally hidden in the depths of the cold blue loch.

'Ach, drat it!' came a voice from behind a rock.

Hamish straightened up and looked around. There was not another soul to be seen, and no other footprint but his own on the smooth wet sand.

'Och, for goodness sake!' came the voice again, squeaky and grumpy like a bad-tempered old man.

'Who's there?' called Hamish, searching around the rocks.

'Who do you think? You daft gomeril!'

Hamish walked right round the rocks. There was nobody in sight. He stopped and look about him, thoroughly puzzled.

'Mind where you're putting your great big feet!'

Hamish looked down, and there behind the rocks lay a huge sea urchin. It was easily the biggest sea urchin that Hamish had ever seen. His great rounded grey and pink shell was covered with crusty knobs and spikes.

'I beg your pardon,' said Hamish. 'I didn't see you lying about down there.'

'Obviously not,' grumbled the urchin. 'That's the trouble with you folk that have feet. Think you can put them anywhere. Ech – humph!' The sea urchin tried to move himself along the rock, but only managed to roll over onto the sand.

'Are you – eh – in trouble?' asked Hamish, politely.

'Well you don't think I'm sitting

around here for fun do you?' said the sea urchin rudely. 'The tide's gone out and left me high and dry. High and dry! I'm trying to get back to the water.'

Hamish stood up and shading his eyes with his hand peered down the loch to the faint blue line of the sea.

'You've a fair wee bit to go,' he said. 'Here let me give you a hand.'

'Aye, well, as long as they're not as clumsy as your feet,' grunted the urchin ungraciously.

Hamish bent to pick him up. The sea urchin was quite taken by surprise, he had never been handled before, and shot out all his bristles.

'Yee-ouch!' yelled Hamish, dropping him and stepping back quickly.

'Clumsy big tumshie,' snorted the sea urchin. 'You're worse than a walrus.'

'It's your own fault,' said Hamish, feeling a bit peeved. 'Can you not fold up your spikes or something?'

The sea urchin sniffed, but he folded his spikes back flat against the shell. Very carefully, Hamish picked him up in his two hands and set off across the sand. He picked his way slowly round the wet rocks, past the pools. As he went the sea urchin moaned and complained all the time.

'Och, be careful, will you,' and, 'mind what you're doing, you great gormless lump!'

'I'm trying to help but you're not making it very easy,' snapped Hamish.

He hurried on, aware now that the tide would soon be turning and the sea would come back in to fill the loch again. Once he slipped on a patch of seaweed and nearly fell. The urchin, shaken up, pushed out all his spikes again.

After that Hamish took off his big blue knitted tammy and carefully lifting the sea urchin into it, carried him like that the rest of the way.

Down to the beach and the water's edge he walked, where the wind was lifting fresh, and the green sea waves tumbled in over each other, crisp and creamy white.

The tide had turned and was starting to come in again.

'Right, laddie,' came a muffled voice from the blue tammy. 'This'll do fine. Just leave me here, and off home with you afore the sea catches you. Quickly now!'

Hamish turned and looked back up the loch to where his wee farm cottage stood, a tiny white speck on the green hillside. Already the sea was washing in over the sand around him, trickling and gurgling round the rocks at his feet, filling up the pools and rippling over the sand. In no time at all he would be cut off.

'How do I get back?' he asked. 'That tide is coming in fast.'

'One good turn deserves another I suppose,' said the sea urchin grudgingly. 'Follow the sands. They'll take you home. Just listen to them – and follow your big feet!'

Hamish stood and listened. Above the sound of the sea and the gulls crying in the wind, he could hear another sound.

There was a soft, gentle singing that seemed to come from around his feet.

'It's the sands,' said the sea urchin. 'They're aye covered with the sea, but they belong to the land. They'll take you back to it. Goodbye now, and thank you.

You're not a bad lad – in spite of your big boots.'

Hamish watched as the wee waves lapped around and over the sea urchin, welcoming him home. Then he turned and walked back across the sand, following the sweet wild singing little tune. Sometimes it seemed to come from his right, sometimes it was to the left of him. But always it was ahead, leading him through the rocks and pools, back towards the white cottage on the hillside. And as he walked the sea rippled in behind him.

At last Hamish stepped from the sand to the seaweed and rocks of the beach beneath his own two green fields. He turned and watched as the water washed away his last steps from the place where no man had ever walked before.

And as he watched, the tumbling waves curled back leaving a beautiful sea shell lying at his feet.

It was pink and white, rounded to the shape of Hamish's two big hands, with a smooth rippling pattern, like the waves on a summer sea.

Hamish shook out the water, held the

shell to his ear, and listened. Far away, as
if from a great blue distance, there came
to him the sound of the singing sands,
leading him home safely to Mirren.

6
Mirren and the Fairy Blanket

Spring had come early to Camusbuie.

Hamish had dug over the warm brown earth, and he and Mirren spent long days working in the garden by the cottage planting cabbages, carrots, turnips and bright summer flowers.

There was only one task left now before summer came, and that was the shearing. Each year the heavy grey winter coats that had kept the sheep warm through the dark freezing months had to be cut short. This done, Hamish took the sheep back up the hill to the high summer pasture while Mirren prepared the fleeces and spun the wool that would make warm clothes for the next winter.

'This year,' said Mirren as she washed the thick soft fleece, 'I shall make us a fine new blanket that will hold us warm and snug through all the long cold nights.'

'Grand idea,' said Hamish. 'And make it long enough so that my feet don't stick out at the bottom of the bed!'

On Monday morning, as soon as Hamish had left for the high pasture, Mirren set to work.

The fleeces were tangled and matted and she sat by the fireside with her two wooden carding bats, pulling the wool backwards and forwards through the spikes, teasing out the knots. Mirren brushed and pulled, brushed and rolled until at last she had baskets full of fine soft fluff, all ready for the spinning.

On Tuesday, Wednesday and Thursday Mirren sat at her spinning wheel, drawing the white fluff into a strong thread. She twisted and spun the thread onto wooden bobbins. And as each bobbin filled with the soft thick strands of wool, Mirren replaced it with an empty one. She sang as she spun.

'Hurrum, hurrum,
Turn, wheel, turn,
Spin a bonny bobbin,
Turn, wheel, turn.'

Day after day the wheel turned, until at last all the bobbins were full.

Then Mirren lit a fire in the farmyard and set on it a huge iron cauldron full of water. She gathered together mosses and roots and as she stirred them in, the water turned a rich orange colour.

'We must dye the wool,' said Mirren. She took the bobbins and with the help of Hamish's mother wound the yarn into loose hanks. When the pot was steaming and bubbling gently, Mirren stirred in the hanks and left them to soak in the orange coloured water.

When she judged that the first batch was ready, Mirren fished it out of the hot water with a stick and spread the hanks to dry on the spiky fingers of the gorse bushes on the hillside behind the house. And so she went on winding, dyeing and spreading the golden orange wool to dry in the sunlight.

It was while she was spreading out the third batch that Mirren noticed that some of the first hanks seemed to be missing.

'The wind must have taken them,' she thought. But it was a still warm, windless day.

'Perhaps Hamish's mother has them,' thought Mirren. But the old lady shook her head. She had been dozing in the sunshine by the door.

Mirren counted the hanks of wool on the bushes again. There were fifteen.

'I will leave them tonight,' she said. 'And in the morning we shall see what we shall see.'

In the morning there were only seven hanks on the gorse bushes where the fifteen had been – and there were some long pointed footprints by the bushes.

'So-ho,' said Mirren. 'Now who could this be, I wonder.'

She washed and dyed and spread out a few more hanks of wool, but then instead of going back to her work she hid behind the low stone wall of the garden, and watched and waited.

At first nothing happened. The morning wore on and the sun rose high in the sky. Then just as Mirren was beginning to wonder if it was not after all a great waste of time, a small figure sneaked down the hillside and crept over to the bushes.

She was twisted and bent with straggly hair that tumbled over her face. She wore shoes with long pointed toes and an old dirty green cloak.

She was quite unmistakeable.

'Grizelda Grimithistle!' whispered Mirren. The nasty little witch who had stolen their milk was now stealing Mirren's carefully spun wool.

Mirren watched as Grizelda lifted some of the hanks and tucked them under her cloak. Picking up her skirts she crept back into the thick bracken that covered the hillside above the cottage, and disappeared.

'Hmmm!' said Mirren. 'We'll soon see about this!' Pulling her shawl round her shoulders and lifting her petticoats, she followed Grizelda.

Over rocks and streams went the old witch, her long pointed feet squelching through the boggy places with Mirren following carefully behind. Grizelda stumped on, turning now and then to look back. Mirren, flitting from bush to bush, followed her to the top of the hill, then dropping down on her hands and knees she peered through the long grass.

Beneath her, in a cleft in the hillside, was a small dark cave. By the entrance, on a wooden stool, sat Grizelda. She was knitting with a huge pair of wooden pins and Mirren's orange wool. As she knitted she chanted to herself.

> 'Clicketty clack, clicketty clack,
> It's a fine warm blanket that I'll make.
> And little does Mirren ken, the fool,
> That it's me has stolen all her wool.'

She rocked about on the stool, howling and cackling with laughter.

'Well!' said Mirren. She was just about to jump up and go storming down to the cave when suddenly she stopped . . . and thought.

Everyone knows that fairy knitting is the finest in this world or any other. There is a magic woven into the stitches and secret patterns. A blanket knitted by the Wee Folk is a thing to hold and treasure indeed, and to pass on to your children and their great-grandchildren, for it will bring sweet sleep and good fortune to whoever owns it.

Mirren remembered all this and, re-membering it, slipped off quietly back down the hill, leaving Grizelda to knit her blanket.

All next day Mirren sat carding more

wool and trying to think of a way to trick Grizelda into giving her the finished blanket, and at last the answer came to her.

Before she spun the wool she went out to the farmyard and putting on her fine white Sunday gloves she picked a huge basket full of stinging nettles. As she spun the wool onto the bobbins Mirren bound in the green stinging leaves. Then she dyed the wool as before and left it to dry in the sun.

'Now, Mistress Grimithistle,' said Mirren, 'help yourself – please do.'

Sure enough when she looked again next morning the wool had gone.

Two days later Mirren crawled through the long grass to peer down at Grizelda again. All the hanks of orange wool had been knitted up into a huge square blanket and the old witch was just finishing off the last corner.

As she worked she chanted to herself.

> 'Clicketty clack, clicketty click,
> I've stitched my blanket warm and thick.
> With spells and magic woven right
> To hap me through the winter's night.'

Then pulling the wool through the last

stitch Grizelda threw down the wooden pins and shook out the big orange square. As Mirren watched she pulled off her dirty old green cloak and wrapped the blanket round her bent shoulders.

'Ooo-ouch,' howled Grizelda.

'Yeeee-eeech,' squealed Grizelda, dancing about in pain. She threw the blanket on the ground and stamped on it angrily.

'That's gey rough wool,' she snarled, poking at it with a long pointed toe. Then she lifted the blanket again, shook it hard and wrapped it round her shoulders again.

'Aaaa-oooo!' yelled poor old Grizelda, as the nettles stung her back. Tearing the blanket off she hurled it away down the hillside.

'I don't know what kind of sheep they have,' she snarled. 'But I'll not trouble to steal their wool again!' She grabbed her cloak and stamped off into the cave.

Mirren tiptoed from her hiding place, and trying not to giggle too loudly bundled up the blanket and hurried home.

Once again she put the big iron pot on

the fire, filled it with water, and pushed in the blanket. Then she took a stout stick and sang as she stirred and pounded.

'Stir and row, stir and row,
That will make the nettles go.
Grizelda's knitting soon will be
Safe and warm for Hamish and me.'

And sure enough the green stinging nettle leaves floated to the surface of the water, leaving the wool soft and smooth. Then Mirren carried the blanket to the gorse bushes where she spread and stretched and smoothed out the tiny fairy stitches with the dream charms and sleep spells knitted through the wool.

In the evening, when the blanket was dry and warm, and perfumed by the wild flowers of the hillside, Mirren carried it carefully into the cottage and laid it on her bed.

When Hamish came home she told him and his mother about the trick she had played on Grizelda Grimithistle.

'I would never have thought of that myself,' said Hamish's mother smiling and shaking her head. 'My, Mirren, but I think you're the cleverest one of us all.'

'Did I not tell you that?' laughed Hamish, hugging Mirren and dancing her round the kitchen.

And in the tiny white painted bedroom the Fairy Blanket glowed like the sunset of a perfect summer night, so that ever after Mirren and Hamish knew sweet sleep and enchanted dreams.

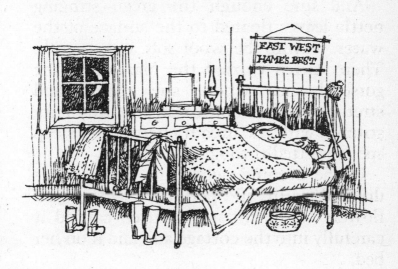